16.89

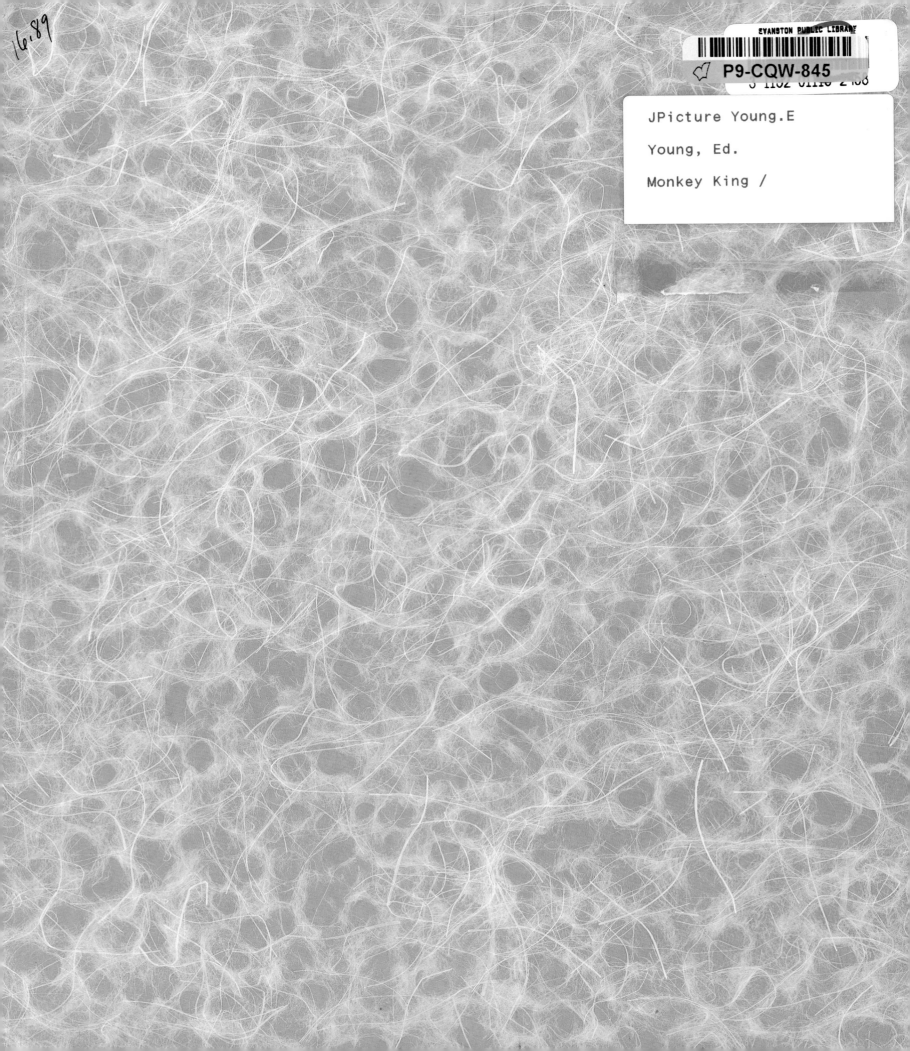

Ed Young
Monkey King

HarperCollinsPublishers

Monkey King

Copyright © 2001 by Ed Young

Printed in Hong Kong. All rights reserved.

www.harperchildrens.com

Library of Congress Cataloging-in-Publication Data is available.

ISBN 0-06-027919-2

ISBN 0-06-027950-8 (lib. bdg.)

The collages in this book were made with a mixture of handmade and bought papers.

The text was set in 28-point Cochin. The display type was set in Bitstream Freeform 721 Bold.

Typographic design by Joy Chu

1   2   3   4   5   6   7   8   9   10   ❖   First Edition

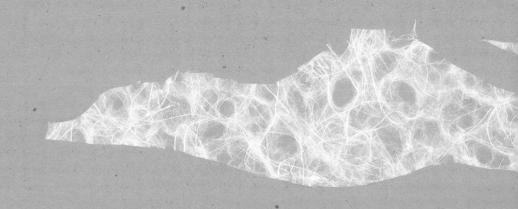

TO URSULA, FOR HER INTEGRITY AND CONVICTION,
WHICH PLACED QUALITY ABOVE PROFIT

Once upon a time,
on a faraway island
off the coast of
ancient China, a
rock exploded on
Flower Fruit
Mountain.

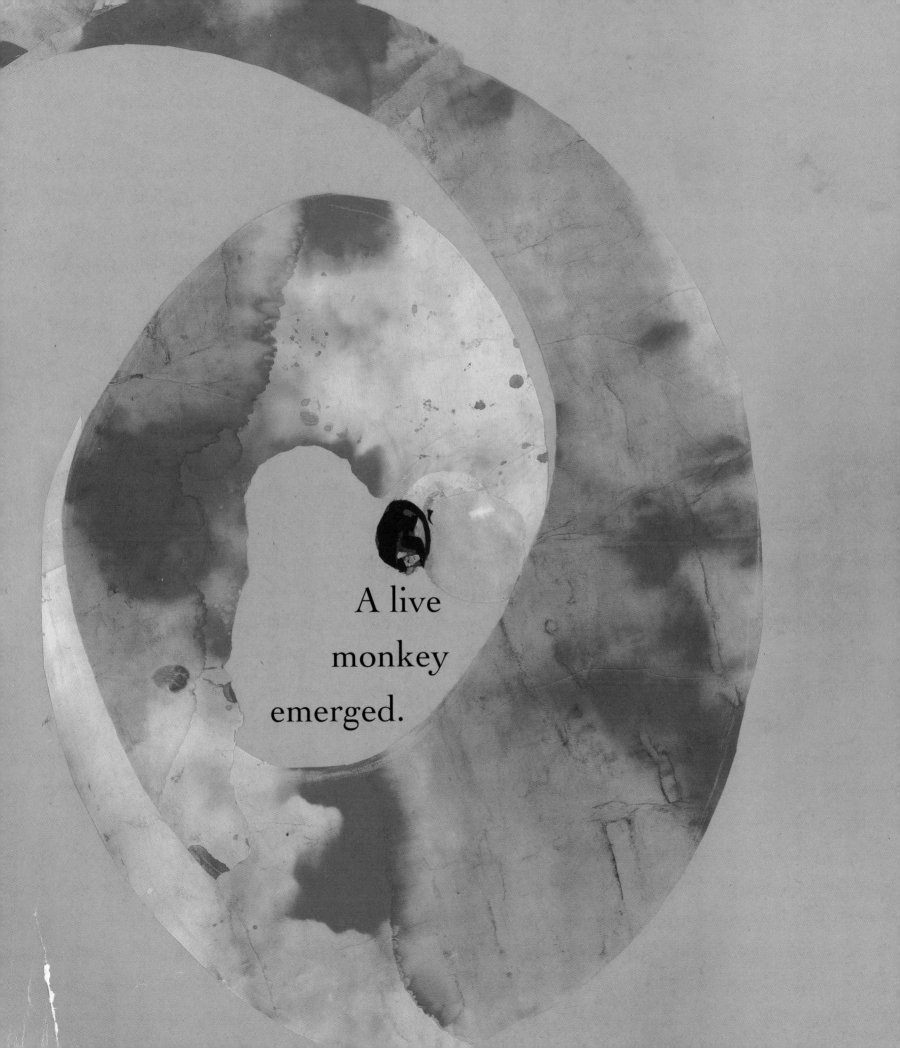

A live

monkey

emerged.

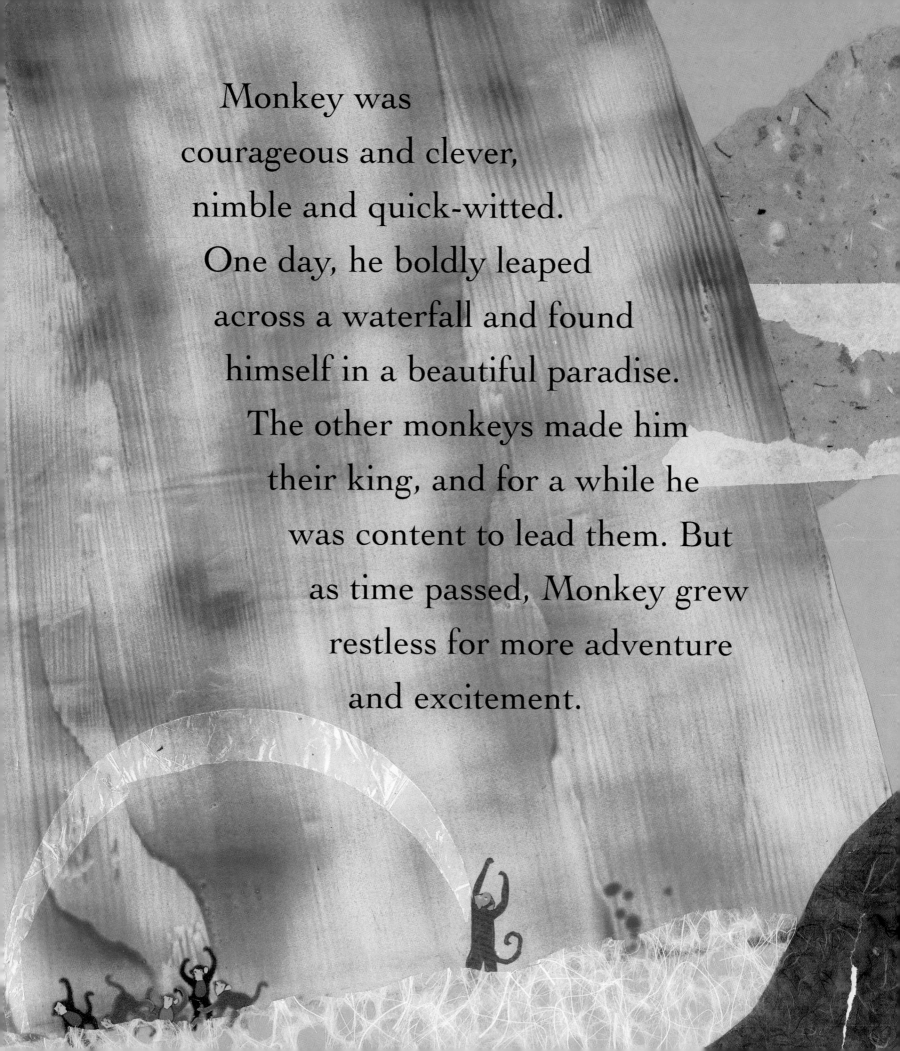

Monkey was
courageous and clever,
nimble and quick-witted.
One day, he boldly leaped
across a waterfall and found
himself in a beautiful paradise.
The other monkeys made him
their king, and for a while he
was content to lead them. But
as time passed, Monkey grew
restless for more adventure
and excitement.

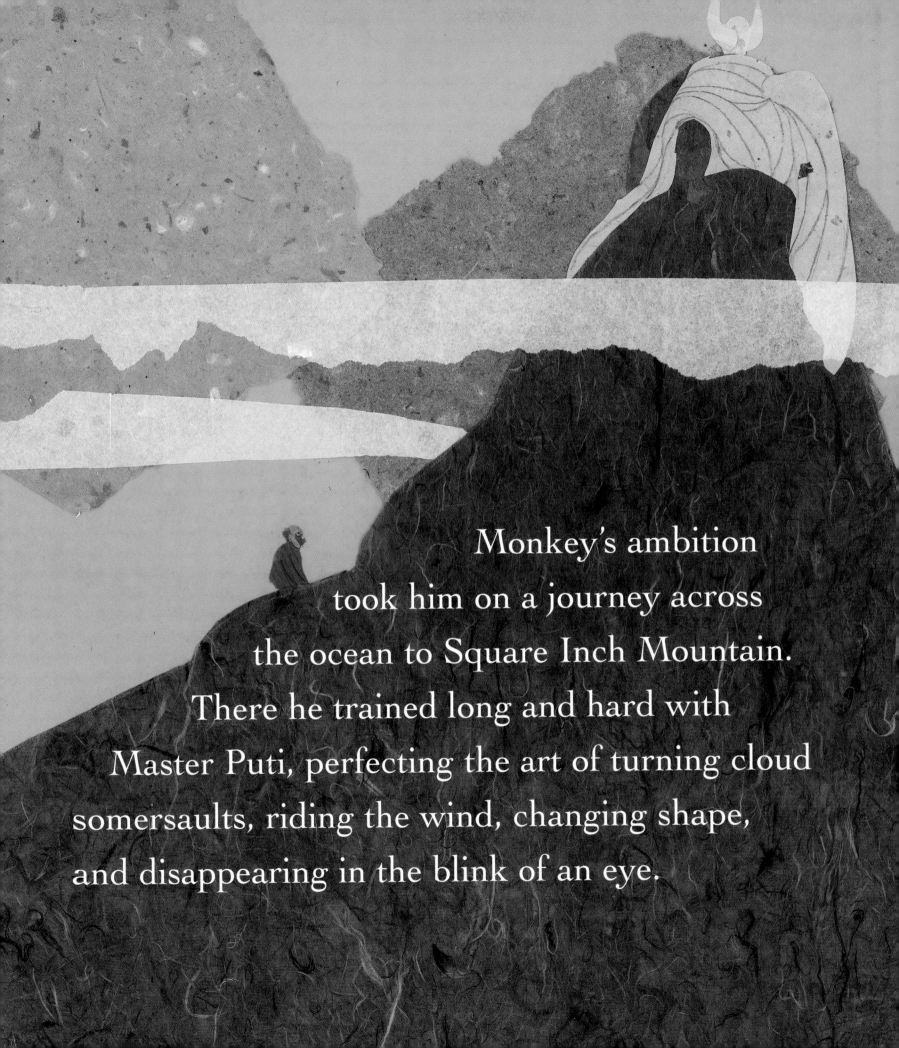

Monkey's ambition
took him on a journey across
the ocean to Square Inch Mountain.
There he trained long and hard with
Master Puti, perfecting the art of turning cloud
somersaults, riding the wind, changing shape,
and disappearing in the blink of an eye.

Hundreds of years passed before Monkey returned home. He arrived at Flower Fruit Mountain just as Red Beard Bandit was invading his kingdom.

Monkey threw himself
into the fray. Using his magic
tricks, he speedily dispatched Red Beard.

Monkey thought he deserved a weapon that was truly worthy of a hero such as himself. He found a gold pillar in Dragon King's underwater palace. As soon as he saw it, he had to have it.

He shrank
the pillar until
it was as small
as a needle,
and he tucked it
behind his ear.

Then he took a
running leap and
somersaulted
home.

When Dragon King complained about Monkey to Jade Emperor, the emperor decided to keep an eye on Monkey. So he offered to make Monkey his Minister of Stables.

Monkey was delighted—until he discovered that he had been given one of the lowliest jobs in heaven! Monkey was so hurt and angry. He plucked all the forbidden fruit from the immortal peach tree and gobbled them up. Then he tumbled home before anyone could punish him.

Jade Emperor sent his top generals after Monkey,

but Monkey divided himself into one hundred tiny monkey soldiers and forced the generals to retreat.

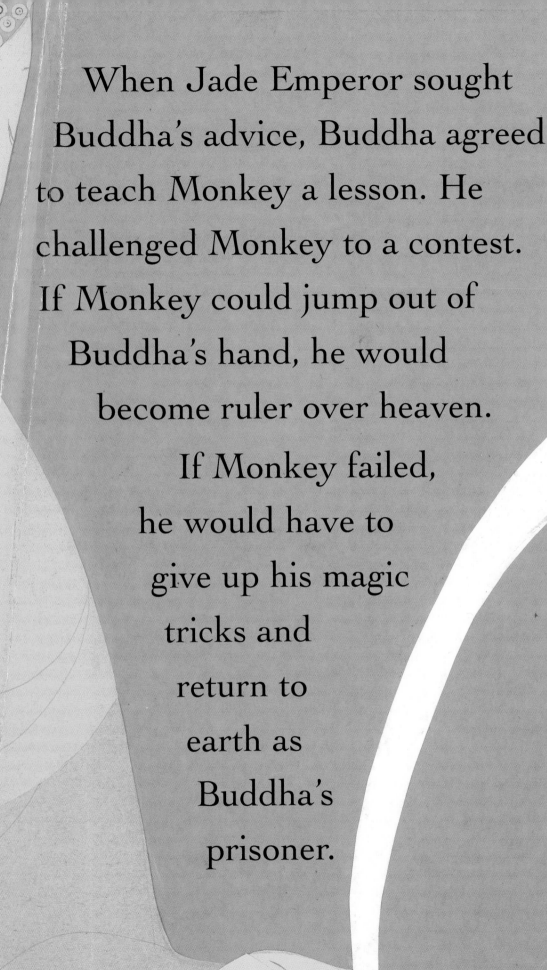

When Jade Emperor sought
Buddha's advice, Buddha agreed
to teach Monkey a lesson. He
challenged Monkey to a contest.
If Monkey could jump out of
Buddha's hand, he would
become ruler over heaven.

If Monkey failed,
he would have to
give up his magic
tricks and
return to
earth as
Buddha's
prisoner.

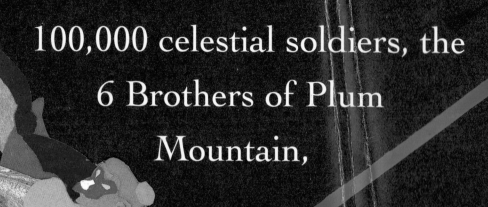

100,000 celestial soldiers, the 6 Brothers of Plum Mountain, and 36 thunder generals.

Still, no one could capture Monkey and his miniature army.

Next, Jade Emperor sent his prince leading an army of

"Nothing to it," thought Monkey, "when you have an amazing somersault trick like mine."

In a flash, he leaped into the air, tumbling over and over again across the expanse of heaven until he came to five columns.

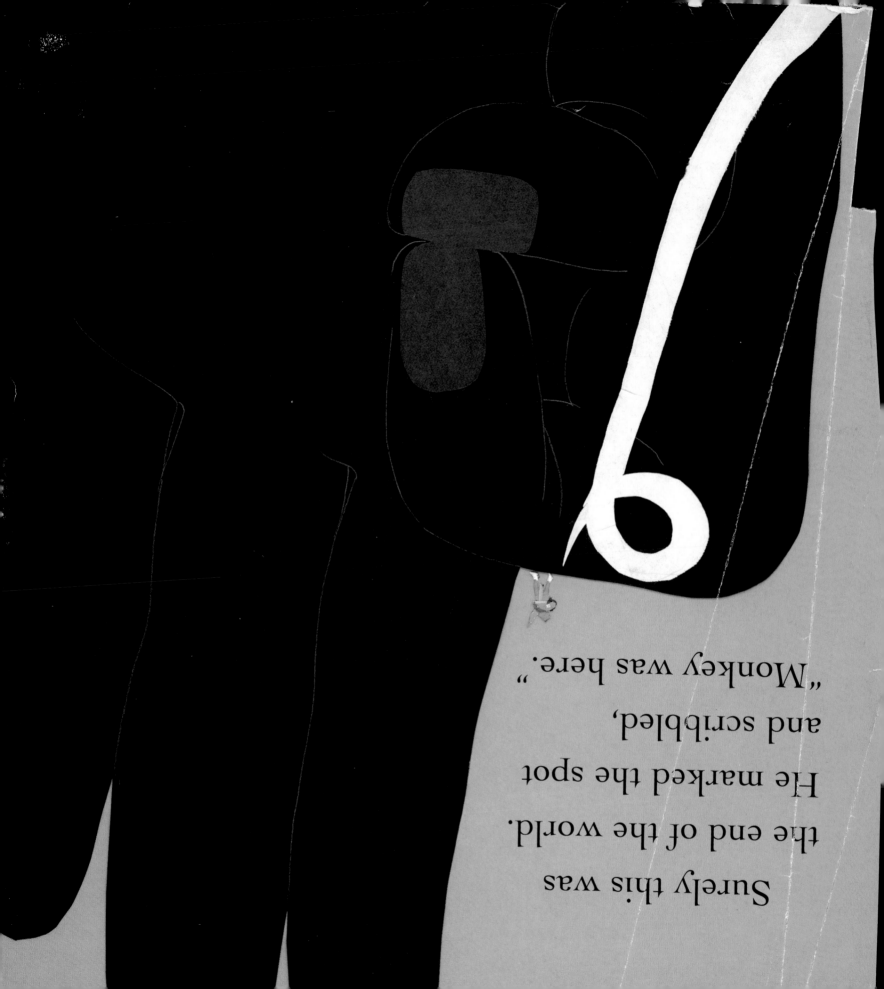

Surely this was
the end of the world.
He marked the spot
and scribbled,
"Monkey was here."

But Monkey was not at the end of
the world. He was trapped inside
Buddha's hand!

Instantly, Buddha turned his
hand into the ridges of Five Finger
Mountain and trapped Monkey
under a boulder. Monkey lost all
his magical powers.

For five hundred years,
Monkey lived in captivity,
contemplating his past misdeeds.

One day,
holy monk Tang
passed through
Five Finger
Mountain.

He had been sent on a
dangerous journey to the west in
search of Buddhist scriptures. When
Monkey agreed to serve as his
disciple, Monkey regained his
freedom and his powers.

Monkey tried to keep out of trouble,
but it wasn't always easy to stay good.

One night, Monk Tang
and Monkey arrived at
a large temple.

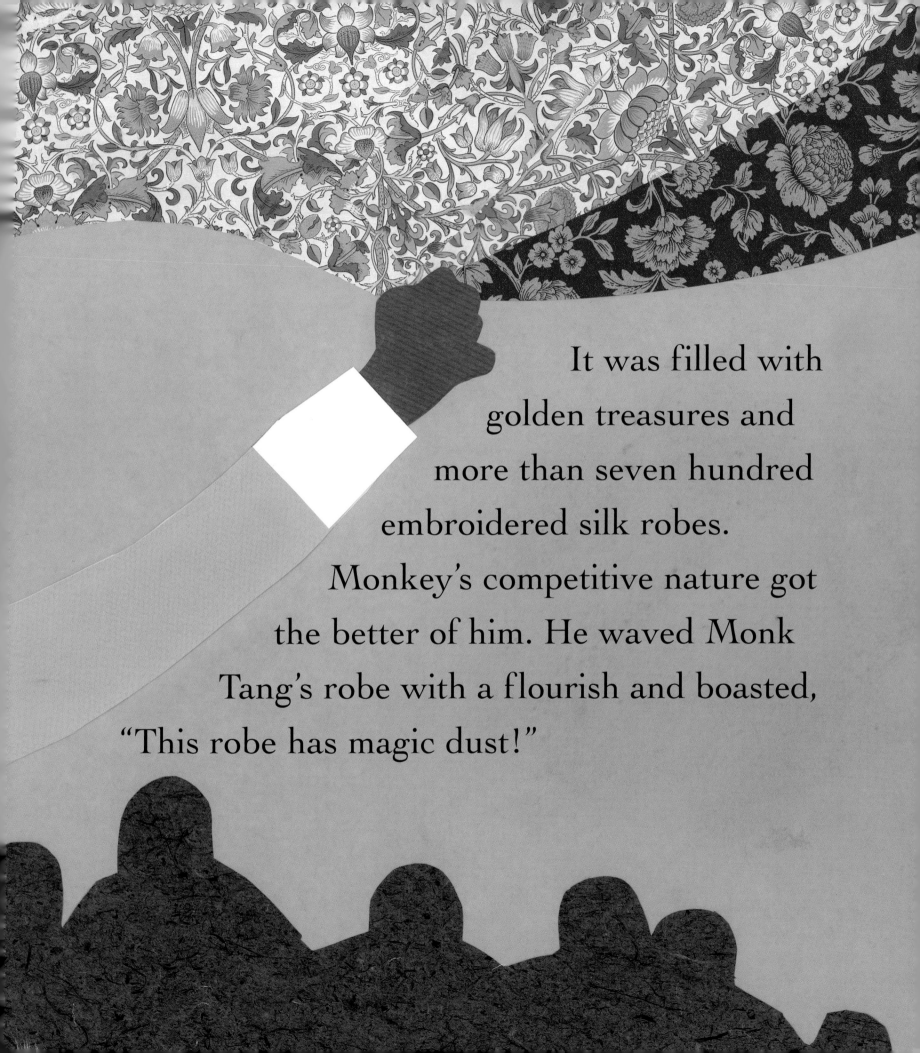

It was filled with golden treasures and more than seven hundred embroidered silk robes. Monkey's competitive nature got the better of him. He waved Monk Tang's robe with a flourish and boasted, "This robe has magic dust!"

Now, the chief priest of the temple was a greedy man. As soon as he saw the robe, he wanted it for himself. That night, while everyone slept, he stole it and set the temple on fire.

Luckily, Monkey was a light sleeper.

He changed into a bee
and whizzed into action.

He cast a spell
upon Monk Tang
that made him fire-proof.
Then Monkey retrieved
the robe and placed it on the
roof for safekeeping.
Monkey fanned the flames of the
fire toward the main hall of the
temple, not caring if the monks and
the temple burned up.

Over on Tornado Mountain, Black Bear saw the fire. He raced to the temple but was distracted by the glittering sparkle of Monk Tang's robe. He swallowed it up in one gulp and hurried back to his cave.

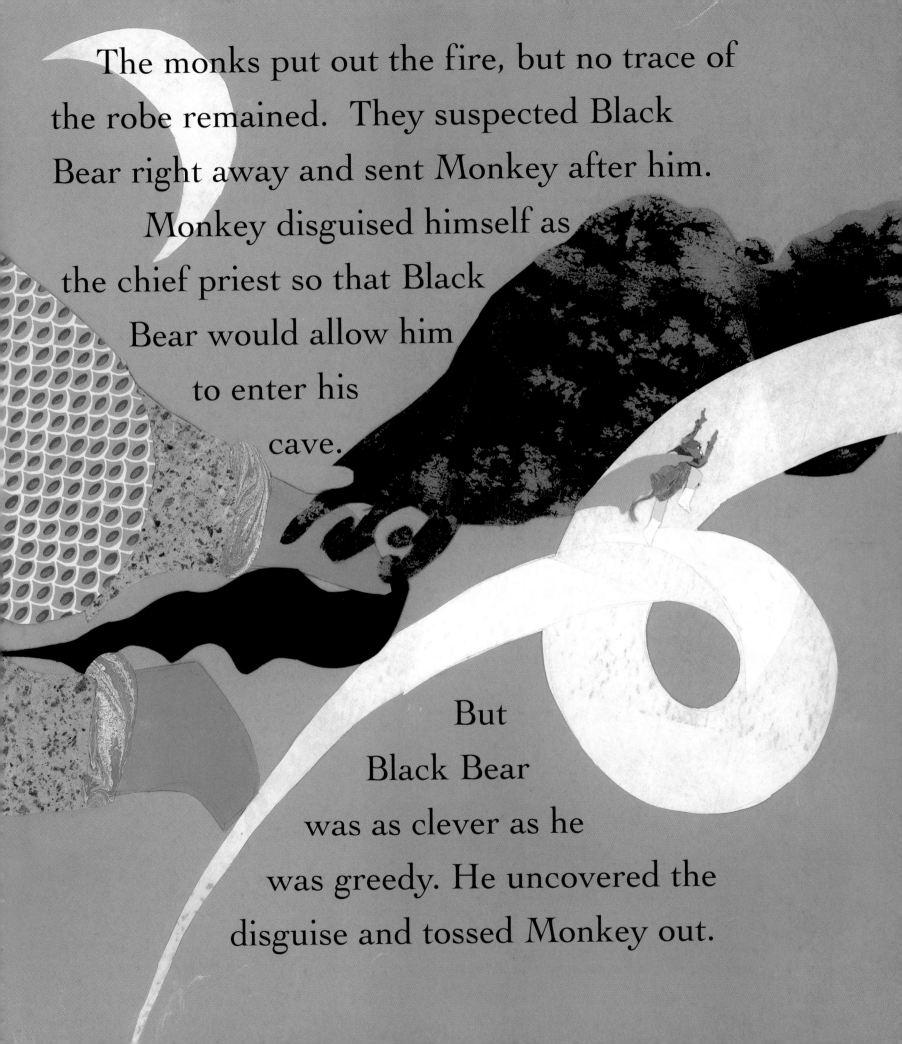

The monks put out the fire, but no trace of
the robe remained. They suspected Black
Bear right away and sent Monkey after him.
Monkey disguised himself as
the chief priest so that Black
Bear would allow him
to enter his
cave.

But
Black Bear
was as clever as he
was greedy. He uncovered the
disguise and tossed Monkey out.

For the first time, Monkey was willing to ask for help. He jumped on a cloud and flew to heaven, where Guan Ying, the Goddess of Mercy, lived.

Guan Ying felt sorry for Monkey, so she changed him into a long-life pill and persuaded Black Bear to swallow it.

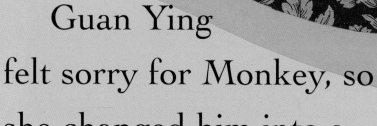

Once inside Black Bear's belly, Monkey kicked and punched so hard that Black Bear, in desperation, promptly spit out Monkey and the robe.

Monkey returned the robe to Monk Tang, and they continued their journey under Guan Ying's protection. By learning that there was strength in admitting to weakness, Monkey had saved the day. Did Monkey's humility last? That's another story for another book.

AUTHOR'S NOTE

The Chinese epic *Journey to the West* comprises the entire journey of Monkey and his companions toward a more enlightened state.

The adventure saga is set in T'ang dynasty China (A.D. 618–907) during the rule of T'ai Tsung, who was emperor from 627 to 649. It is believed that in 627, the sage monk Tang Tsen started his journey to India to bring Buddhist scriptures to China. In the story, Tang Tsen travels with a white horse and three disciples: Monkey, Pig, and Water Demon. By heavenly decree, the horse and disciples were serving penance for their misdeeds by protecting the monk from wicked mortals such as the greedy chief priest at the temple and beasts such as Black Bear.

The subtext of this great literary work reveals a deeper spiritual journey toward enlightenment, salvation, and Buddhahood.

The disciples try to be faithful servants to the monk, but their human foibles lead them astray from time to time. Monkey is an impulsive trickster hero, but he is also courageous and loyal, carefree, joyous, curious, and impetuous, just like his brother and sister monkeys. Pig and Water Demon, who do not appear in this story, are greedy and short-tempered, but they too have positive attributes.

This adaptation attempts only to introduce the very beginning of the classic tale, as well as Monkey, perhaps the most colorful character of the cast.

A List of Characters

MONKEY is clever and courageous, with an appetite for mischief and showing off.

MONK TANG, also known as Tang Tsen, was a devout Buddhist. He lived from 596 to 664.

JADE EMPEROR, the ruler of Heaven, is depicted as weak and cowardly in the Chinese epic *Journey to the West.*

GUAN YING is the Goddess of Mercy and Compassion. People pray to Guan Ying for help and understanding.

BUDDHA is the most powerful deity of the Buddhist religion.

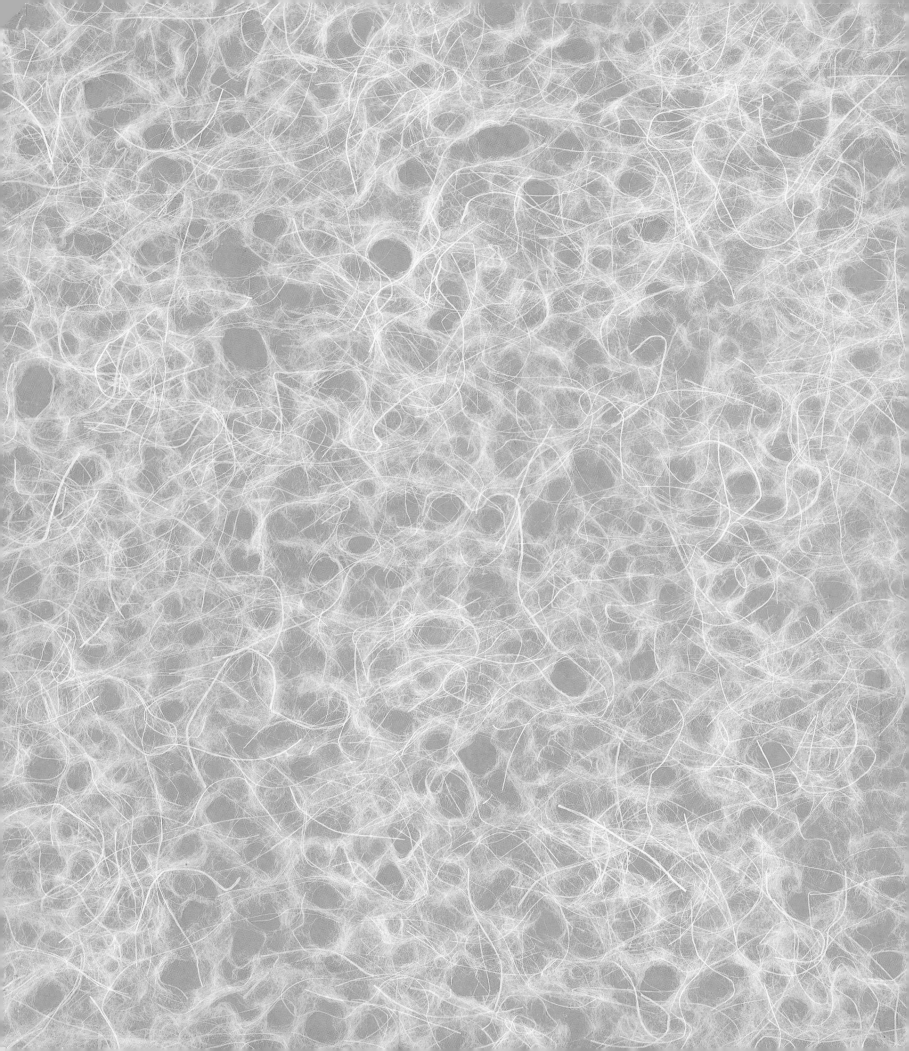